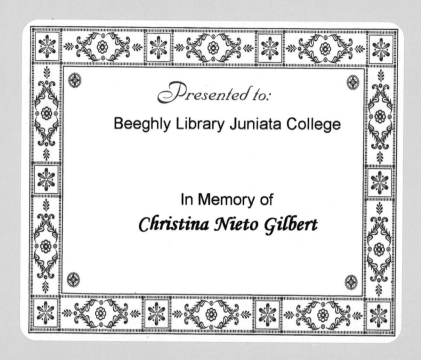

Presented to:

Beeghly Library Juniata College

In Memory of
Christina Nieto Gilbert

Daisy and the Doll

For information about permission to reproduce
selections from this book, write to

PERMISSIONS
THE VERMONT FOLKLIFE CENTER
MASONIC HALL
3 COURT STREET, BOX 442
MIDDLEBURY, VERMONT 05753

LIBRARY OF CONGRESS | CATALOGING-IN-PUBLICATION DATA
Medearis, Michael.
    Daisy and the doll / by Michael Medearis and Angela
Shelf Medearis ; paintings by Larry Johnson.—1st ed.
        p. cm.—(The family heritage series)
    "A family heritage book from the Vermont Folklife Center."
    Summary: Daisy, an eight-year-old black girl living in rural
Vermont in the 1890s, is given a black doll by her teacher and
becomes uncomfortable that her skin is a different color from
that of her classmates, until she finds the courage to speak from
her heart.
    ISBN 0-916718-15-8 (hardcover)
    1. Afro-Americans—Juvenile fiction. [1. Afro-Americans—
Fiction. 2. Self-esteem—Fiction. 3. Prejudices—Fiction.
4. Dolls—Fiction. 5. Schools—Fiction 6. Vermont—Fiction.]
I. Medearis, Angela Shelf, 1956- II. Johnson, Larry, 1949- ill.
III. Title. IV. Series.

PZ7.M512745 Dai 2000
[Fic]—dc21   00-024597

ISBN 0-916718-15-8
Printed in China
Distributed by Independent Publishers Group (IPG)
814 North Franklin Street, Chicago, IL 60610

FIRST EDITION

Book design: Joseph Lee, Sue Yee, Black Fish Design
Series Editor: William Jaspersohn

10 9 8 7 6 5 4 3 2 1

Publication of this book was made possible by grants from the
Fund for Folk Culture and the Christian A. Johnson Endeavor Foundation.

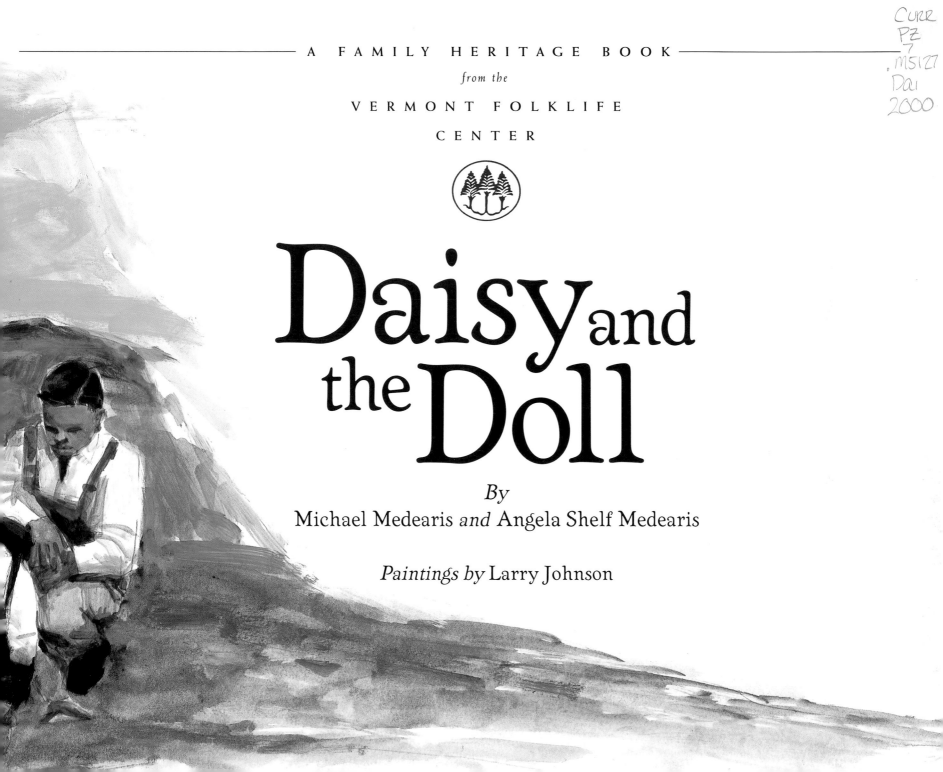

A FAMILY HERITAGE BOOK

from the

VERMONT FOLKLIFE

CENTER

Daisy and the Doll

By

Michael Medearis *and* Angela Shelf Medearis

Paintings by Larry Johnson

My full name is Jessie Daisy Turner, but everyone calls me Daisy. I am eight years old and the middle child of thirteen children. We live on a farm in Grafton, Vermont. From my window I can see the fields of beautiful daisies I was named for.

My favorite time of day is after our chores are
finished and we've eaten dinner. Then, my daddy
and my momma—Papu and Mamu—and my
Uncle Early tell stories and sing songs. We all
take turns making up poems, even the children.

On Saturdays, our neighbors come over and we square dance the night away. Sometimes Papu lets me call out the steps.

I go to school in the village. Every Monday morning, my teacher, Miss Clark, makes special announcements.

One day she said to us, "Class, as you know, Friday is the last day of school. This year, for the end-of-school program, we are going to recite poems about all the different countries and nationalities from around the world. There will be a prize for the best speaker. I want this to be the best program we've ever done."

Miss Clark passed out slips of paper to everyone and gave each girl a doll to carry in the program. She handed me a rag doll with a coal black face. Some of the girls giggled a little when they saw my doll.

"Your doll's name is Dinah," Miss Clark said. "And here's the poem I wrote for you."

I read the poem over and over. Anger bubbled inside me like hot tar. As soon as school was out I ran home.

Papu was busy clearing a field of tree stumps. When he saw my tears, he wrapped his arms around me.

"What's the matter, Daisy?" Papu said.

"Everyone laughed when they saw the doll Miss Clark gave me," I said. "And here's the poem she wants me to recite."

Papu read the poem and we sat quietly for a long time.

"Daisy," Papu said. "Look at all the flowers and trees out here and tell me which one is the prettiest."

"They're all beautiful, Papu," I said.

"My dear little Daisy," Papu said, "when I look at you I see the prettiest girl in Grafton, Vermont. You can present your black doll in the program and be just as proud as anyone else. Now go on and memorize your poem."

Papu gave me a hug and I hugged him back. As I walked up the hill to the house, something became clear to me. I had never really noticed the color of my skin. It was as if Miss Clark's poem had opened my eyes for the first time.

My father, my brothers and my sisters are a variety of colors, from a pale, butter-colored yellow to a rich, dark mahogany. My mother is almost as white as Miss Clark. Skin color had never been important to me—until that day.

The last week of school seemed to fly by. I tried hard to practice the poem Miss Clark had given me. But the words seemed to stick in my throat.

"Daisy Turner!" Miss Clark scolded. "You are usually so good at reciting poems. Do you think you'll be able to say your part tonight?"

I just nodded my head. I felt sick at the very thought of saying that poem.

That evening, almost everyone in town crowded into the schoolhouse. My class sat in the front row. I was the last one in line. Every girl except me was dressed in her best frock. I wore an old red school dress. For the first time in my life, I felt ashamed of the way I looked.

Miss Clark gave a short welcome speech and introduced the two contest judges. They took their seats on the stage.

Amy Davis was first on the program. She smiled at the crowd as she cradled her doll in her arms and said:

> *My dolly came from sunny France.*
> *Her name is Antoinette.*
> *She's two years old on Christmas Day,*
> *And a very darling pet.*
> *I hope she'll take the prize.*

Amy twirled her skirt as she walked across the stage. She sat down and gently placed Antoinette on a chair in front of her. One by one, my classmates recited their speeches and sat on the stage. The crowd clapped loudly and cheered at the end of each poem.

Finally, it was my turn. My feet felt like lead
as I walked to the center of the stage. I hung
my head and stared down at my shoes. I tried
to say the words Miss Clark had written, but
they caught in my throat like a bone. Someone
coughed. It sounded like Papu. I looked out into
the crowd. His smile warmed me like the sun.
I took a deep breath and stood tall, just like the
pine trees that surround our house.

I started reciting a poem, but I did not say the
verses that Miss Clark had written. Anger
turned my voice to a high pitch.

You needn't crowd my dolly out,
Although she's black as night.
And if she is at the end of the show,
I think she'll stand as good a chance
As the dollies that are white.

Miss Clark turned red. She stood up as if to stop me from speaking. Papu rose and started down the aisle. I was scared, but the words continued to pour out of some deep place in my heart.

My Papu says that half the world
Is nearly black as night.
And it does no harm to take a chance
And stay right in the fight.
So sit up, dolly!
Look hard and straight
At the judges on your right.
And I will stand close by your side,
Though I do look a fright.

When I finished, everyone stared at me in shock. A strange silence filled the room as I took my seat. It was as if the audience was holding its breath. The two judges whispered to each other for a long time. Then the judge named Mr. Beck peered at me over his glasses.

"Daisy Turner, come forward," he said. I felt like I was walking underwater as I moved to the center of the stage.

"Miss Turner," Mr. Beck said, "that was the most original and honest presentation we have ever heard on a children's program. You let us know just how you felt. You are the winner of the end-of-school program. Here is your prize."

He reached into his pocket and handed me a ten-dollar gold piece. Everyone stood and applauded, even Miss Clark. They were all clapping for me!

On the way home, I held the gold piece in the palm of my hand. It glittered in the light.

"You just keep right on speaking the truth, Daisy Turner," Papu said. "You'll do just fine."

"I will, Papu," I said. I snuggled next to him and cradled Dinah in my arms.

"You know what, Papu?" I said. "Dinah looks a little like me."

"Well, so she does," Papu said. "And that's what makes her the prettiest little doll in Grafton, Vermont."

RHYME TIME

When Daisy Turner was a little girl, there were no radios, TVs, movies, computers, CD players or VCRs. For entertainment, Daisy and her family often told stories, played word games and made up rhymes and poems. As you saw, Daisy could instantly make up a poem even while standing on a stage in front of an audience of adults!

How about you? Can you make up instant rhymes and poems?

One way to get warmed up is to play the following rhyme game. You can play it by yourself or with others—though it's most fun playing it with others.

Here is a list of words to get you started:

pie, cat, star, hay, deer, bear, book, bone, pain, blue, pocket, lip, crow, jump, hot, fish

Tell Me a Word

Players sit in a circle and one player says, "Tell me a word that rhymes with _____," and he says a word. Then, one by one, each player has five seconds to call out a word that rhymes with it. For example, if the first player says, "Tell me a word that rhymes with 'bake,'" the next player might say "cake," the player after that "rake," the player after that "flake," and so on. If a player can't think of a rhyming word, he or she is out. The winner is the last person left.

A Rhyming Poem

Now, all by yourself, think of a subject you like and write a rhyming poem about it. Your poem can be about anything—your pet, a family member, a season, a favorite relative, a holiday, an animal, a planet—anything! Try to make your poem at least two lines long, and longer if you can. Try to make the last words in each pair of lines rhyme. For example:

**My dog named Ginger loves to play
With a tennis ball on a rainy day.**

Have fun with the rhymes. When you've finished your poem, read it to your family. Then take a bow. After all, you're a poet. Daisy Turner would be proud of you!